"For readers Pacific, it's a natural. For those without such a background, it can also be compelling since the pathos doesn't really depend on island life, more on war time conditions in a Japanese possession. What was especially effective was the sparse entries in the diary, something so much in keeping with the characters in the novella. Well done!"
- Francis X. Hezel, S.J., Micronesia Seminar

"I have recommended *Miss Gone-overseas* as supplementary reading to many of my students... Among the book's many virtues, it so gently presents a nuanced view of the gendered and complex relationships between Japanese settlers in Micronesia and the people they encountered there."
- Greg Dvork, Associate Professor of Asian and Pacific Islands Cultural Studies, Hitotsubashi University, Tokyo.

MISS GONE-OVERSEAS

(Karayuki-san唐行きさん)

A Pillow Book by

Mitchell Hagerstrom

Penryn Editions

MISS GONE-OVERSEAS
Karayuki-san 唐行きさん

Copyright © 2019 by Mitchell Hagerstrom
2nd Edition

Published by PENRYN EDITIONS

Penryn.editions@gmail.com

The author would like to thank *Latte* where a portion of the novella first appeared in a slightly different form. 1st Edition published in 2012 by Tiny Toe Press.
Cover photo, courtesy of Kurt Bell

ISBN: 978-1-7330086-0-0

AUTHOR'S NOTE

From the late years of the 19th century until World War II, it was common for Japanese companies to recruit girls and young women for overseas jobs in nursing or clerical work. They were called Karayuki-san, or Miss Gone-overseas, as it translates. Most, but not all, were actually sent to work in commercial brothels. These years were the heyday of Japan's vast colonial empire in Southeast Asia and the Western Pacific.

The particular young woman who narrates this book was born in the early 1920s in a mountain village west of Tokyo, raised and educated there. When she was eighteen, her family arranged a marriage for her with a young man in a distant mountain village. He was soon drafted for the war in China and only a short while later became a casualty. His new bride became an unwanted widow. As such, his family sold her to a broker who resold her to a Tokyo brothel which later transferred her to Nagasaki and from there to one of the Caroline Islands of Micronesia. When she arrived on the island, American forces were beginning the push through the Marshall Islands, toward the Carolinas, toward the Marianas, then to Tokyo and the Japanese mainland. Her island of Ponape was one of the islands the American military leap-frogged, and no invasion force ever landed.

In the mid-1950s, Japan ended legal prostitution. Street walkers were still allowed, but commercial brothels were shut down. The sex trade went underground. Even today those in the business have to wiggle around the laws, i.e., the famous "love" hotels and massage parlors which are technically not brothels.

I chose to write this narrative as a pillow book, a genre that harks back to 10th century Japan when it was favored by court ladies who kept small day-books in the hollow of their pillows. Night-book is a more apt description than day-book, and several famous ones are still in print. They are not diaries, in the western sense, as they included poems, anecdotes, descriptions of people, clothing, gardens, festivals, along with catty gossip. Later in the 20th century the pillow book genre was revived by high-end call girls and used for keeping notes on the sexual preferences and practices of their favorite customers. Please consider that my use of the pillow book genre for Miss Gone-overseas is a touch of irony (forgivable, I hope) as she was neither a 10th century court lady nor a high-end call girl.

Mitchell Hagerstrom   Austin, Texas 2019

In this floating world,
There are many meetings and
partings.

Li Shang-yin
[9th cent.]

November 1942
The District Center

We have been separated. Kimiko, who slept so sweetly against me on the long voyage, who became like a sister, lovingly calling me Mieko-chan, is in another house. Mrs. Okata is in charge here. She seems a decent sort. I have never heard her scolding someone without reason.

Although it is still dark, birds have begun to sing, and I can hear the foreign voices of the servants rising from the kitchen. Josefa calling for her daughter to hurry, and Sefina whining in answer. Morning will be here soon.

***

The Ifumi is a small house with only five rooms upstairs. Izumi, Chikako, Sumiko, Yukio, and me, each of us has a 3-mat room upstairs although we sleep together below in the 12-mat room. Downstairs is a Western-style parlor and the 12-mat room that opens to the garden at the back. There are also two wings. One has the kitchen, the servant's room, and the bath, the other has Mrs. Okata's room, her office, and the storeroom. The garden is narrow and rather dull, a tangle of plants I do not recognize. Behind the back fence is the water catchment tank and a place laundry is hung to dry and where wood is kept for heating the bath.

The town is less primitive than I expected. It has modern things like telephones, electric lights, and automobiles. The main streets are wide and lined with shops and eating places. There is even a department store where I bought this notebook, almost the same as those I lost. A nice surprise.

***

Remembering back to the day we arrived, the ship coming closer to what we thought was another large cloud on the horizon, then the cloud lifting, and we could see towering peaks covered in vegetation so dark it seemed almost black. Most forbidding looking. I expected a true south sea island with palm trees and beaches, like pictures I have seen.

It was late in the afternoon when the ship passed through a channel in the reef and anchored near a small island in the lagoon. When the boat came to take us ashore, the clouds loosened a terrible downpour and the careful bundle I had made for my notebooks became thoroughly soaked. All that is over now. There is no point weeping over the loss.

***

The heat here can be even more oppressive than summer in Nagasaki. Some days the powder slides down my face and down my neck. It helps that the rooms have ceiling fans.

A large mango tree beside the bath house is the home of many birds who begin their songs well before dawn and some mornings they are so loud I cannot sleep as long as I would like. Chikako and Sumiko say that after a while I will get

4

used to it. Still, bird song is better than
city noise.

***

Always the clouds sitting on the
mountain peaks. Always the rain,
sometimes so fierce that it turns day into
night and makes such a thunderous
sound on the metal roof that all normal
conversation is impossible. We never leave
the house without an umbrella.

The air is very humid and filled
with the stink of rotting breadfruit. It falls
to the ground and lies there. I'm told no
one eats it except the natives in the
countryside. It looks and smells like
something that should be fed to pigs.

***

We are told that our ship will be the
last for a long time, perhaps until the war

is over. It left two days ago, taking home wives and children of the colonists. We went down to the dock to watch as the small boats ferried the departing ones out to the ship. So many tears, so many flowers.

I watched, in particular, a man say goodbye to his son, a very pretty boy about six years old and apparently motherless, as he was entrusted to others who were leaving. Watching the father with his son, I could not keep the tears from my own eyes.

***

One morning last week the governor general made a formal visit. He arrived without warning and as there was no time to change into suitable clothing we were presented in *yukata* and soft sashes. Impossible to look decent dressed like that, but Mrs. Okata lent me a pretty fan.

According to the other women of the house, the governor general has no real power or function now that the island is administered by the military. They say he spends most of his time visiting one house or another. It seems odd that he did not choose to return to the home islands.

***

The soldiers wait their turn in the western-style parlor. Most, however, have gone first to a place where they drink cheap spirits. I believe the Ifumi used to be a tea house, but Mrs. Okata does not serve refreshments. She does allow them to play the phonograph while they wait. Once upstairs they do their business quickly, like rabbits or roosters, knowing the others are waiting.

Most mornings we are free to walk along the waterfront road or up and down *Namiki dori*. A pretty name, but it has no trees. Still, the shops and eating places are shaded by wide overhangs and we can walk almost the whole length in the rain without getting wet. But it is a strange town with hardly any women or children. Other than the natives, of course.

***

The governor general and Mrs. Okata have become fast friends. They spend many afternoons in the 12-mat room, the Go board between them, and one of us must be in attendance to pour his *sake*. Thank goodness all he wants is to talk and drink, because he is so fat we would be crushed.

Josefa, the native woman who cooks, is also very fat while her daughter, Sefina, is very skinny. Mrs. Okata is always scolding Sefina for being so slow. Sometimes Mrs. Okata threatens to sell her to one of the Korean brothels, and

Sefina twists up her eyes like she thinks that might be a good idea. What a stupid girl.

***

The Koreans here do such necessary tasks as operating the crematorium and collecting the night soil. This is because native men are not allowed in the town after dark. They also work in the canning factories. The governor general says the natives are not to be trusted.

The Korean brothels are at the edge of the mangrove swamp where the air is very unhealthy. The women are never free to take walks and their only clients are foreign workers and the very bottom of the soldiers.

***

Kimiko says that when the doctor came to her house, the Oichi, he found one woman with trouble in her lungs. She has been removed to the hospital. She is someone who has been here many years.

When the doctor came to the Ifumi, he said we were all in fine health, but cautioned us against washing our hair on rainy days. And when, I wanted to ask, would we ever see a whole sunny day?

***

The Ifumi has been quiet. Yesterday I went to see Kimiko and she says an alert has been called because Admiral Yamamoto has been killed, his plane shot down at some islands far to the south. She knows this because the Oichi is frequented by those from the naval headquarters.

Today I sat in attendance for the governor general and listened as he told

Mrs. Okata that England is the troublemaker, that it is the English with their tariffs who destroyed our silk industry. They want to keep the China colonies only for themselves. He whispers, too, that the Germans are just as bad, and not to be trusted. Strange how he drinks so much *sake*, but he never laughs.

***

Still the alert, and again last night there were no soldiers. Mrs. Okata sent a planter to my room and he stayed the whole night. Unlike the soldiers, he did not hurry. He kept his eyes shut tight. I suppose he was pretending I was his wife. He must miss her very much.

Planters and the district center shopkeepers do not visit often. Maybe they do not like to wait in the parlor with the soldiers who are so loud and drunk. Also, it is possible they have native women out in the countryside.

***

We have learned that the woman from the Oichi has tuberculosis. She has been moved to the other hospital, the one in Ohmine for those with infectious diseases. Mrs. Okata says the woman must have slept with wet hair and reminded us again of what the doctor said.

Now that there is an empty place at the Oichi, I asked Mrs. Okata if I could move there, and what a scolding I received. I had only thought of being near Kimiko. I did not mean to be ungrateful and everything else Mrs. Okata accused me of.

***

Josefa's sons are fishermen. Besides reef fish sometimes they bring lobsters and for this they must walk out on the reef at night carrying lanterns. The lobsters are small but very tasty.

When I asked Josefa why her eyes are pale green and not brown, she said it is because her father was a German. She says the Germans were here before the Japanese, and before that there were the Spanish, who built the stone wall with the arch we must pass under to reach *Namiki dori*, and before that there were English and American whaling ships and missionaries. Josefa says that someday the Japanese will leave just like all the rest.

***

Finally, I gave my old notebooks to Josefa to burn. I had hoped that once they dried, some of the pages would be readable but none were. The photograph of my brothers is badly damaged too, but I cannot part with it.

When Mrs. Okata called for me to sit in attendance during the governor general's visit, I told her I did not feel well. In truth, I was too ashamed of my appearances, my eyes all swollen from crying, which I had promised myself I would not do. I don't know whether to put away the picture of my brothers and never look at it again, or to make myself look at it every day until I can do it with no tears.

***

Yesterday the governor general took me for a drive in the country. We saw the little train that brings produce from the other side of the island, and from the plantations where coconuts are harvested for copra. The road was so bad we did not go as far as the rice fields or the pineapple plantations.

The corporal, who is the governor general's driver, is very young, not much more than a boy. I could not help but notice that the governor general walks funny. He kicks his legs out in front of him as if trying not to become entangled in his skirts, which looks so comical when he is wearing trousers.

***

One of the soldiers was very drunk last night, so drunk he could do nothing and that made him angry, so he slapped me and that made me angry and I refused to be of any help. Then he burst into tears and left. I heard him stumble on his way down the stairs. Good riddance.

Then, when I wanted to look at my face where he slapped me, my hand mirror was missing. While searching for it, I discovered that two of my favorite combs are also missing. An awful evening.

***

Often now, the governor general stays long into the night. I pour his *sake* and listen as he and Mrs. Okata talk. When they speak in soft voices and when the rain falls softly, I find it difficult not to fall asleep. The others act disagreeable when I do not have to receive visitors, even though sitting in attendance is not something I have asked for. They say I am favored because I am the youngest and because Mrs. Okata and I came on the ship together.

The hand mirror has returned. Chikako had borrowed it, but my combs are still missing.

***

Last night the governor general told Mrs. Okata about a family of Belgians who are spies for the Americans. They have been here since German times and are now under house arrest so they cannot get to a secret radio they have hidden up in the mountains.

He also talked a long time about the war. He said that the Americans want to take our colonies. What business is it to them, these islands of the Pacific? Of course, I said nothing. I am only there to pour the *sake*. Still, it is puzzling that the Americans are so against Japan having colonies when they don't care that the British have them. The governor general said we would never have gone to war if the Americans and the British had kept to their own part of the world and left China and the rest of Asia to us.

***

Another alert has been called. The governor general says it is nothing to be alarmed about, merely practice for when the Americans come, though he says they will never come to this island because the harbor is too small. The ships of the Imperial Navy are kept at the next big island, one with a large, deep lagoon.

Mrs. Okata is having the garden weeded by Josefa's sons. They would be handsome if they weren't so dark. The ginger is in bloom, like bouquets of white and yellow butterflies, the scent so strong it makes me giddy.

***

They say that the roof of the Nambo Department Store is a pleasant place in the evening, that a cool breeze comes off the lagoon and people have a merry time. I have asked the governor general to take me there. He has agreed but will not say exactly when.

Yesterday there was a trace of lipstick on Sefina's mouth. I suppose it was she who took my combs. I am told that out in the countryside the native women go bare-breasted, like savages. Here in town they prefer to copy the style of Japanese women and you see many fashionable gold teeth in their smiles.

***

Last night we put on our best western-style dresses and had a party just for ourselves. We played records in the front parlor and danced. Izumi is very good at boogie-woogie. We had such fun and are not looking forward to the soldiers coming off alert.

Most of the evening Mrs. Okata wore a sour look that reminded me of one of my old schoolmasters, Mr. Ito, and several times she complained that we were being unpatriotic. Still, she did not make us stop and was seen tapping her fan on her knee in time with the music.

***

The Emperor was sent from Heaven to lead our nation, Mrs. Okata reminded us, and because she insisted, we went to the shrine to make amends for our disrespectful party. It was raining so hard we could not take the shortcut up the side of the hill but had to go around the long way and before we arrived, we were soaked up to our knees. Then, on her way up the steps Sumiko stumbled and cut her hand. Mrs. Okata gave her a scolding for being so clumsy.

At the shrine I remembered my husband who was killed in China, and my brothers who are now soldiers and who might also be killed. We all prayed loudly, following Mrs. Okata's example, asking forgiveness for our unpatriotic behavior.

Yesterday Kimiko and I walked to the end of *Namiki dori*, then past the agriculture station and beyond before turning back. Kimi-chan is the youngest of all of us. Like me, she comes from the country and remembers the same childhood things, like the harvest festivals and capturing fireflies on summer nights.

On the way back, we stopped to buy some mosquito coils but there were none to be found. We were told that the ship, the one we came on, brought mostly supplies for the soldiers, and we were reminded that there may not be another ship until the war is over. Kimiko bought a new umbrella, then we went to the Nambo where I bought another notebook, bottle of ink, and a replacement nib for my Pilot, even though steel is supposed to last a lifetime.

***

Mrs. Okata is angry because Yukio and Izumi have had their hair cut and fashioned into finger waves. She prefers for us to look old-fashioned. But Yukio and Izumi say it's so much cooler, that it dries so much faster, and we're all crazy not to do it, too.

Mrs. Okata also scolded Chikako, for what reason I do not know. Now, Chikako is even more gloomy than usual, so I gave her a box of face powder to cheer her. Anymore, I only bother to wear powder when the governor general visits.

***

Mrs. Okata has turned out Yukio and Izumi. Now, there are only Chikako, Sumiko and myself, and Mrs. Okata has forbidden us to wear western-style dress. I think she has gone slightly mad. This morning her *fusuma* was partially open when I passed and I saw her sitting in bed, her hair loose, waving her arms as if she were dancing, and crooning a funny song about grasshoppers.

Yukio and Izumi have been taken in by another house and there are whispers that Yukio intends to go live with a planter in the country. I have heard that several women from other houses have left to live with planters whose wives have gone back to the home islands. Everyone knows that if the Americans come it would be much safer to be living in the countryside.

***

After promising so long ago, the governor general took me to the roof of the Nambo. There I saw the man who I had seen saying goodbye to his son, that pretty child. The governor general said the man is an engineer and is in charge of the hydroelectric plant.

Because the engineer has a certain resemblance to elder brother, I have been remembering back to the day my husband left for China, remembering elder brother showing the same kind of sadness I saw when the engineer said goodbye to his son, though it was at a train station and a winter day without flowers. But that time, too, there were many tears on everyone's faces, except mine. Until elder brother's wife pinched me hard. He had only been my husband for a few weeks and had been extremely unpleasant the whole time.

***

When I asked the governor general why he did not choose to leave on the ship that took the others home, he said Japan is not a good place for younger sons. I suppose it is because the governor general is so big that I never considered he could be a younger son.

He then confided to me that the ship did not go to the home islands as planned, but instead landed all the passengers on the island of Saipan for the duration of the war. He says no one is to know this as it would be bad for the colony's morale. I am to keep the secret. Everyone must continue to believe the ship went all the way to the home islands.

***

Today Josefa packed us *bento* boxes and we walked to the river to bathe and have a picnic. There has been no rain for almost a week and the catchment is getting low. The river is small but has been dammed to make a bathing pool.

Just as we began to disrobe, some soldiers appeared out of the bushes and sat themselves down to watch us, but Mrs. Okata chased them away with a stick. We laughed in our sleeves at the sight and decided that Mrs. Okata must have been a fierce *samurai* in a past life. Then Sumiko said she must have done something awful, to have come back as a woman.

***

Yesterday Chikako slapped Josefa for bringing tea, when it was something else she asked for. When Mrs. Okata heard this, she gave Chikako a terrible scolding and sent her away. Sumiko told me that Chikako had asked for *sake*, not tea. Now there are only Sumiko and myself.

I have been remembering how relieved my parents were when I married. Some in the village were beginning to whisper I was an old maid. I remember how proud my parents were that they had made such a good marriage for me. But nothing has turned out as they expected. How unhappy they would be if they knew.

***

Still no rain, the dust flies in the streets and settles inside on every surface. There is an epidemic of pink-eye. The governor general is suffering from it and does not visit. Yesterday Sefina's left eye was swollen shut and today Josefa sent her home to the country. The catchment is so low that we can only take splash baths from a bucket. Mrs. Okata has locked the front door and says she will keep it locked until the rains return.

Leaves are drying on the trees. When the wind rattles them, it sounds like autumn. The house feels quite empty now.

***

Last night I woke thinking I heard rain, but it was merely dry leaves and twigs falling on the roof, a wind with no rain. Sumiko and I now sleep behind a screen in the 12-mat room.

Sefina has not returned from the country and her brothers only bring small reef fish. Josefa says it is no longer allowed to use lanterns for night fishing or to take a boat out beyond the reef. Often now we have tinned beef with our rice. Josefa says there are few vegetables in the market.

***

Today we made a trip to a larger river to bathe. But we had to walk far to find an agreeable place with a deep pool. Where we turned off the road, we could see the roof of the engineer's residence. The hydroelectric plant is higher up the side of the mountain. But even in the mountains there is less rain, so the hours of electricity have been cut.

We brought with us clothing and bedding and spent the afternoon as washerwomen. With the sun and the heat, everything dried quickly, and we returned before dark.

***

At night soldiers rattle the locked door and call out curses when no one comes to open it. In the dark they cannot see the sign Mrs. Okata has nailed there that says quarantine. When she first put up the sign the doctor came to see about it, but she refused to let him in.

Whenever Josefa has green papayas, she makes a substitute for pickled vegetables with lime juice and grated ginger. Vegetables will not ferment properly in this climate. There are only a few tins left in the storeroom. I will mourn

when there are no more pickled plums.
Many clouds, but no rain.

***

Last night, a night with no moon, I
woke to screams filling the dark, such
terrible screams I could feel them on my
skin. And my own screams, too. At first, I
thought they were all my own screams,
until Sumiko shook me and made me
understand that the screams were from
Mrs. Okata's room. We hurried across the
passage.

No one else came, but of course
how could they with the front door locked
tight. Still, even Josefa did not come. We
lit the lamp and when Mrs. Okata was
quiet, we lay down, each beside her, until
dawn.

***

Mrs. Okata will not speak of her nightmare. She is still terrified, and we cannot leave her side. Sumiko agrees that it is better not to press her, that in time she will forget.

Better, too, for me not to remember back to that other black night, the night of the child who did not want to be born, and the blessing of the doctor arriving with chloroform. Later they told me the child had been born dead and that more children were not possible. Foolish thoughts, all that is past.

***

This morning Josefa announced there would be rain before evening, and there was. Sumiko and I ran out into the garden and let it pour over us. Our clothing still dripping, we woke Mrs. Okata, but even the rain did not cheer her. She sleeps all day and sits motionless as a

Buddha all night with the lamp lit. Sumiko and I must sleep with our sleeves over our faces.

The governor general sends his driver, the young corporal, every day to inquire after Mrs. Okata, and every day we must tell him there is no change. The soldiers no longer knock at the door. It is surprising that no one, that is no one in authority, has come to demand she unlock the door.

***

Now that the rains have returned there is again electricity all day and well into the evening. Sumiko and I went out for a walk this morning for the first time in a long while. Many of the small shops along the waterfront road are closed because there is no more merchandise. *Namiki dori* was almost deserted.

We also went to the Oichi, but when I asked for Kimiko, I was told that she has disappeared. They said she has been missing for over a week, that perhaps she has gone to live with a planter. It seems strange that she would do this without confiding such plans to me.

***

The weather has been stormy, more rain than I could ever imagine possible. The garden is flooded, and the floor of the bath is slippery with slime.

This afternoon I saw Josefa leaving Mrs. Okata's room carrying a small bundle. She showed it to me, it was Mrs. Okata's hair. Sumiko was upset, though she would not say why, and left the house, saying she would send for her things tomorrow. Mrs. Okata gave no reason for cutting off her hair, or for Sumiko's leaving, but she seemed almost cheerful.

When the corporal came, she wrote a message for him to deliver to the governor general.

***

Kimiko has been found, hanging from the rafters of a small house on the outskirts of town, her beautiful hair wrapped round and around her neck. They say a young naval officer took and kept her there. The neighbors heard her screams but said they did not dare to interfere.

I hate this wretched place of younger sons and soldiers. Is this war the fault of the English and the Americans, as the governor general says? Long before this war, Japan sent young farmers to die as soldiers in China. Kimi-chan's limp was barely noticeable. She should never have been forced to come here.

***

Over a month has passed since Josefa left. The corporal no longer drives the governor general as the military has taken his automobile. So, the governor general stays here. He and Mrs. Okata play Go in the 12-mat room. All day and much of the evening there is nothing but the click of the stones and the murmur of their voices.

Today the corporal brought back some fish, but I refused to cook them. They were old, rotten, and the stupid boy gave too much for them. I buried them in the garden and was ashamed that he saw my tears.

***

I have learned to cook rice over a coconut husk fire as it seems wise to save what kerosene we have. There are still many sacks of rice and crates of *sake* in the storeroom, some condiments, but little else. The corporal goes out every morning to see what he can trade for. But people are more and more unwilling to barter away their food, even for a pretty lamp or a perfectly good *futon*. I'm sure he would have more success trading with the *sake*, but that of course must be saved for the governor general.

All afternoon and most of the night, the click, click of the stones and the governor general calling for more *sake*. He calls for the corporal -- *iiko, iiko* -- who sleeps on one of the sofas in the front parlor. The corporal is a good boy, but that is not a nice way to call someone.

***

When elder brother's wife gave me the choice between this life or returning as a burdensome widow to my parents, did I not make the choice myself? How could I return to my father's farm when all the looms were idle and me another mouth to feed?

Kimiko had no choice, her parents sold her because no one would marry a cripple.

***

I have always wondered if perhaps there was a child. If it had been a girl, they would not have hidden it from me, but put us both out of the house. Perhaps it was a son, which elder brother's wife sent out to nurse until I was gone.

When my husband was killed, they kept the news from me for months, afraid it might cause me trouble, or rather, trouble for the child I carried. Of course, thinking about all this, changes nothing.

***

The corporal has cut off his trousers at the knees, he says he can wade in the tide pools better. His skin is getting quite dark and he seems happy to go to the lagoon each morning. I wish I could go with him someday.

Mrs. Okata has grown thin because she will not take more than tea and scanty bowls of rice, even though I scold her. The governor general is still fat, although he too eats very little.

***

This morning, while the governor general and Mrs. Okata were sleeping, I went to the front parlor and shook the corporal awake. I made him to understand that we must be very quiet, then I put a record on the phonograph and turned it very low. But how can you teach someone to dance who is made of wood!

After my husband left for China, elder brother's wife forced from me the confession that during our short time together he had not done his duty. She told me that since she had not been able to produce an heir for the family, and younger brother had not performed his duty, I must allow elder brother to come to my room. If he appears unable, she said, you must encourage him. You must take his member like this, she said, and she took my finger into her mouth and stroked it with her tongue.

***

Today, before the governor general's bath, I burned incense, hoping to mask the stink of the privy which has not been emptied because the Koreans have gone to the countryside looking for work on the plantations. The town is more and more deserted.

As I scrubbed his back before soaking, I asked the governor general if we should not also move to the countryside. He said he and Mrs. Okata would decide if it should become necessary. He likes the water heated much too hot for this climate.

***

The corporal returned this afternoon with clams cradled in his shirt front. They were tiny things, not much bigger than my thumbnails. After steaming them, it took forever to separate the meat from the shells, but the governor general and Mrs. Okata seemed to like the result, the little clams swimming in a meager broth. Like peasants, the corporal and I poured our portions over our rice. He and I have begun to take our meals together in the front parlor. I call him my little brother.

Yesterday I set a sleeve on fire, even though it was properly tied back. Now, I am wearing one of the corporal's vests under my *yukata*, so I can drop my sleeves while cooking and then, in only two seconds, can be somewhat presentable again. I only wear cotton *kimonos* and soft sashes anymore unless I have to go out.

***

The corporal and I emptied the privy. It was obvious no one else would come to do it. We carried the buckets into the mangrove swamp. Afterwards, we bathed for a long time, but the retching odor seems stuck in my nose.

The corporal is from Tokyo where his father keeps a small stationery shop. He says he is fortunate to have been assigned as the governor general's driver, fortunate he does not have to live the life of a regular soldier. It would have been most unfortunate if the military had taken the corporal away when they took the governor general's automobile.

***

A cloudy day, but very hot, the air so heavy that breathing is difficult. When I happened to complain of this to Mrs. Okata, she spoke to me for the first time of her nightmare. She said what she felt was a hot black wind sucking the breath from her. And a furry stink, like being smothered by a giant rat. She said she is afraid something terrible is coming.

Is it possible she had a dream of something in the future? Some people have that gift.

***

The corporal says work on the airfield is finished and that the native workers have begun to dismantle the catholic church to use in building bunkers. I suppose this means that the Americans are expected, despite what the governor general says.

Maybe, Mrs. Okata's nightmare was about the Americans coming, though I would rather believe she was only recalling seeing a rat, perhaps when she was a small child and the rat looked so huge and terrifying.

***

The Nambo Department Store is still open. Last night the corporal and I went to the roof for a limeade. We were not warmly welcomed until they saw we had money. The engineer, the one who put his son on the ship, was sitting alone at a far table. The strings of fairy lights were not lit, and the atmosphere was not so gay as before. Still, it was something to do during the long evening hours and I hope we will go again.

The governor general has not been feeling well and complains of pains in his chest. I offered to bring the doctor, but he does not want that.

***

A sunny day. I did the laundry. Then, climbed the hill to the shrine, thinking to offer prayers for Kimiko, but found I could not compose the proper words. Instead I sang a firefly song.

***

For the past three days there has been nothing but rain and high winds. The mango tree, heavy with unripe fruit, came crashing down in the middle of the night and flattened the storeroom of the bakery next door. No one was hurt as the Yamada family has moved to the countryside because there is no more flour and no more ships to bring any more. The noodles they made were even better than their sweet rolls. How hungry I am for a bowl of steaming noodle soup.

The corporal has been unable to go to the lagoon in this weather. The last meat we had was a chicken he captured when no one was looking. Such a stringy old thing that I suspect it may have been someone's pet.

***

Four days ago, the corporal was bitten by a large centipede as he stepped out of the bath. At first, his foot swelled like a paper lantern and he still cannot walk very well. I have gone out myself looking for food, but all I have come back with are coconuts.

We have been careful to measure out only a small amount of rice each day and have many bags left. This seems quite prudent as it may be a long time before the war is over.

***

The engineer in charge of the hydroelectric plant came to visit the governor general. He brought a gift of a large piece of fresh tuna. While they sat talking, I helped Mrs. Okata to her bath, and then she supervised while I prepared the tuna. We gorged ourselves on *sashimi* and I sent a plate in to the governor general and the engineer who stayed all afternoon. The corporal kept them supplied with warm *sake*.

The engineer told us the Belgian prisoners have been moved to a place near the old South Seas Government building, that the move was made for the safety of the town, as it is thought that the Americans will not dare endanger the lives of their spies. But the engineer says he knows the Belgians well and does not believe they are American spies. The governor general agreed. Three of the Belgians are young girls, sisters.

***

When the engineer does not visit, there is again the click of the stones as the governor general and Mrs. Okata sit at the Go board. Several times the corporal has gone to the engineer's house where they give him pumpkins and papayas. We are not getting fat, but neither are we going hungry.

According to the corporal, the engineer is living with a native woman. He has seen her and believes she is expecting a child.

***

Today American planes dropped bombs on the new airfield. The noise was terrifying, and the upper part of the town is on fire. When the bombing began, Mrs. Okata buried her head in her sleeves as if that would protect her. The waterfront road is crowded with those fleeing east. Others, they say, are going by boat to the southwest, to Kitti.

Mrs. Okata has agreed that we must go to the engineer's house on the river, as he has offered and as the corporal and I have been urging for weeks. She must now convince the governor general. The corporal and I are packing the few things we can carry.

February 1944
The House on the River

The corporal has been here before, but in the dark we passed the house completely as it is well hidden by a thick stand of bamboo. Only a narrow path to the door is kept clear. Fortunately, the household heard us and the engineer, who is Mr. Uchida, came out to the road and called us back.

For the governor general it was a difficult journey and he leaned heavily on the corporal's and my shoulders the whole way. Several times he sat down beside the road and refused to go on. I am ashamed to admit that I scolded him harshly. As Mrs. Okata says, it is only because of the governor general's friendship with Mr. Uchida that we are not out in the countryside with no roof over our heads.

***

The house has a proper entrance for the leaving off of shoes and *geta*, then a passage between two 6-mat rooms. Mrs. Okata and I stay in the one that is Mr. Uchida's office. The governor general and the corporal in the one across the passage. The main room faces the river and is large enough for more than twelve mats, but the floor is bare wood as the only walls on three sides are wire-mesh screens. There is no veranda, only two covered walkways, one to the bath house, the other to where Mr. Uchida and his wife stay. The servants are in a small place behind the kitchen which is near the bath house.

Across the road is a garden of vegetables, pineapples, and small groves of papaya and banana trees. Past where the servants stay are more gardens and the privy.

***

Mr. Uchida's wife is called Armina, but I have not yet met her. Mrs. Okata says she is half Japanese, the child of a native woman and one of the early colonists. She was orphaned as a small child and raised by Santa and Gustof who are the servants here. As the corporal said, she is expecting a child.

The house being right on the river, there is the constant sound of water and the cheerful calls of birds in the trees. But when the bombs come the noise is terrifying, even from this far away.

***

The American planes came again yesterday, and we saw smoke coming from the district center. The corporal calls the planes Mr. B., Mr. Bomber. Today, when they had not come by early afternoon, Gustof and the corporal took a cart to the Ifumi. We are awaiting their return. The governor general is still not well. Mrs. Okata and I sit with him by turns.

During the quiet times, I help Santa prepare meals. We are careful to build only small fires, and then, under the trees and hope the smoke cannot be seen.

***

More bombs today, but not for the district center but the airfield to the south. As usual, the big guns on the ridge of Jokehs fired at the planes and as usual none were hit.

Yesterday Gustof and the corporal returned from the Ifumi with bedding, mosquito nets, the governor general's supply of *sake*, bags of rice and other things from the storeroom. They saw many people returning to the district center to dismantle houses and carry the pieces far into the jungle to build shelters. The corporal said someone had stolen the phonograph. Fortunately, Mrs. Okata kept the storeroom locked.

***

More bombs. Mr. Uchida and the corporal walked up the road to a clearing to watch. We are safe here because the planes come from the south and therefore cannot see the hydroelectric plant or this house on the river.

During the bombing, Mrs. Okata went to the south wing and sat with the lady Armina. I stayed with the governor general. He first held his hands over his ears, then pressed to his chest, his lips thrust forward in a pout, eyes squeezed shut. The face of a child about to cry. I think we all feel that way.

***

More fires in the district center and, from time to time, we can hear explosions from places where munitions are stored. I worry about the other women, but Mrs. Okata assures me they are safe in the countryside. Mr. Uchida says the Belgians have been moved to the regular jail which is above us on the river road. I suppose this was done for the safety of the guards.

Even though Mr. B. visits every other day, the governor general repeats that the Americans will not come here, that they will go to the next island where the Imperial Navy keeps many large ships in the deep lagoon.

***

When bringing the condiments and other small things from the kitchen and storeroom a trunk was used, the clothing inside as padding for the bottles. But some leaked and I helped Santa wash the clothing in the river, rubbing it over and over with river sand to remove the stains. I have asked Santa to teach me native words. River is *pillapo*.

The governor general asked for the Go board and stones, but when everything was set up, raised on two cushions as he likes, he merely sifted his fingers through the stones in the bowls and decided he did not feel well enough to play.

***

The household has a small flock of chickens. They forage in the yard and under the house during the day and roost in the trees at night. If I do not open my eyes when I first hear the crowing, I can imagine I am a young girl again waking in my parent's house. Soon my mother will call: lazy, lazy, get up! There is work to be done! But when I open my eyes, I see through the mosquito net the woven palm of the sliding screen not the design of maple leaves on the *fusuma* at my parent's house.

Such a long way I have come from that small village. My husband's village was larger. His family sent me to Tokyo, and that house sold me to the house in Nagasaki, and then, the long sea voyage.

The quiet of this place on the river is only disturbed by the noise of the bombings, week after week. When will it end?

***

Mrs. Okata's hair is growing back. Just after washing and before she smooths it down with coconut oil, it stands up all around her head like a thistle blossom. She has begun to leave off wearing a small towel on her head.

The lady Armina keeps to the south wing. If I am in the main room when she passes on her way to the bath house or the privy, she hides behind the sleeve of her *kimono*. Always the one of dark crimson silk. Her hair is very thick and abundant and reaches far down her back. She reminds me of someone in a fairy tale, an enchanted princess, perhaps.

***

When I take up this pen to write, I think of the man who gave it to me. Such a generous gift. I had told him about being a schoolgirl and one teacher who let the students choose to work on their favorite subjects. He let me spend hours on composition and writing instead of math. Anyway, I had hoped the man's gesture meant he would become my patron. But that happens only to fancy *geisha*. Instead, I was sold to the house in Nagasaki and I never saw him again.

The noise of the planes, the bombings, leaves my brain feeling empty. My thoughts fly from me. Sometimes the planes come at night. However do they find us in the dark?

***

The floors of our sleeping rooms are covered with pandanus mats which can be carried out and aired on sunny days, hung alongside the bedding on the walkway railings. Still, we must be careful to keep the shutters closed when it rains and to open them wide on sunny days.

When we lived in the district center, I had not noticed the night sky. Here we have no electricity and go to bed with the sun and rise with it in the morning. But we must sometimes go out in the dark, to the privy. I have never known such dark moonless nights, not even as a child. The sky here has more stars than I have ever seen in my life.

***

I have been told that there is no one else along this side of the river, except for the jail with the Belgians and their guards. The day of the first bombing, when we turned south at the river, other people fleeing warned us that we must go farther out into the countryside to escape. But I feel quite safe. There have been no visits from Mr. B. in almost a week.

Mrs. Okata says that it will not be long before the child is born. She says the lady is very fair and her face quite pleasant. I do not understand why she will not meet me. Yes, I am a brothel worker, but for that matter, so is Mrs. Okata.

***

Returning from working in the lower garden, I saw a flash of color in the garden across the road. It was the lady Armina. As I passed, she fled deeper into the banana grove. I could not help but notice the bold combination of her deep red *kimono* against the pale green leaves of the banana trees.

An idle afternoon. Remembering cherry trees in bloom and I cannot help but compare. Here, across the river a large acacia tree is in bloom, the color of an autumn *gingko*. And there are some trees on the grounds of the protestant church with blooms the color of wisteria, and near the Spanish wall are some giant flamboyant trees whose blooms are the color of fine vermillion lacquer-ware.

***

The bombing has returned but only once or twice a week and always the airfields to the south and west. Again, the click of the stones as Mrs. Okata and the governor general sit at the Go board.

When there is no bombing, living here is like living in a different country. Mrs. Okata has put a piece of colored silk over the telephone that never rings, like a cloth over a dead man's face.

***

Today the child was born. When told it was a girl, Uchida-san did not seem disappointed and said he was pleased because, being a poor man, he had nothing to give to a second son. At that, the governor general cleared his throat, as if to say something of importance. I sensed he was about to tell the secret, that the boy is not safe in the home islands as his father believes.

Fortunately, at that moment Uchida-san left the room. Still, I gave the governor general a scolding, saying we must not give Mr. Uchida additional worries, that putting up with all of us is more than enough. The governor general made a sour face. He said I have become a terrible shrew.

***

Gustof has a small boat that he hides near the bridge and the corporal goes with him to fish in the lagoon. From all the time he spends in the sun, the corporal is getting darker and darker.

Most evenings there are small reef fish with our rice and in the mornings a broth made from seaweed and fish bones. Always we have fruit and croquettes when Santa kills a chicken. But only the corporal is fast enough to catch one.

**

During the afternoon, while the governor general and Mrs. Okata sit at the Go board, Uchida-san reads or looks through papers. I sit across the table from him with my sewing, mostly repairing tears from working in the garden, especially around the pineapple plants.

I no longer wear the vest the corporal gave me, but I often slide my sleeves down and tie them in front, under my arms. When working in the garden, the

63

sun feels good on my shoulders. Mrs. Okata, to my surprise, has said nothing. I expected a scolding.

***

Today, when I was cleaning the floor of the main room, the governor general began complaining of the room being un-matted. When I answered that mats would not be practical as the room has no shutters to keep out the rains, he only grunted and then refused to move, so I had to mop around him. Then, he asked for Mrs. Okata, saying it was past time for her to set up the Go board.

He reminds me of a grumpy old parrot, like the one at Mr. Shimba's *geta* shop: disagreeable, rude, rocking from side to side, and ruffling its feathers. The parrots here are small and not so colorful.

***

A young naval officer was sent to inquire about the hydroelectric plant. When told it had not been damaged, he demanded that Uchida-san restore power to the naval headquarters which somehow survived all the bombing. I heard Uchida-san explain that the request was impossible because the lines are down, and the supply depot was bombed so there is no more line.

I could hear their conversation quite clearly as I was under the house looking for eggs. Santa breaks an egg over the governor general's rice every morning to give him strength. As I listened, I thought: is this the one who took Kimiko away?

***

We bathe in the river in the early evening before the heat of the day is gone. I do not like to go far out into the deep pools as I am afraid of eels. I have never seen fish in the river, but the eels are quite large. Still, we cannot eat then because Santa says they are taboo. But young eels are so tasty! What an ignorant superstition.

Only the governor general, Armina, and Mrs. Okata use the bath house. I have not yet seen the child.

***

Another bombing, the first in a long while, and the governor general is dead. Not from the bombs, but from a heart attack. The bombs were not from American planes as before, but from ships. Though it lasted only a little over an hour, it was much louder than the other bombings.

I had walked up the road with Uchida-san and the corporal to watch. None of the bombs came near here, they

66

were all for the district center. As we were returning to the house, Mrs. Okata came running to meet us, to tell us about the governor general.

***

The corporal and Gustof could dig only a shallow grave because of all the stones in the ground. Uchida-san had them gather more stones and pile them on top. The marker is almost waist high. Terrible that there was no one to read the *sutras*. Not at all a proper funeral. Of course, the crematorium in the district center is no more.

Uchida-san says he is no longer sure the Americans will not come. Now, every sound is frightening, the sudden call of a bird, the wind high in the trees, and all I can think of is the Americans coming.

***

67

The seven-day observances for the governor general, and the American ships are gone. Perhaps, as the governor general always said, they have gone to the next island to do battle with the Imperial Navy. Again, I can go about my garden chores without fearing that every dark shadow in the bushes is an enemy soldier.

Our own soldiers are bad enough. Today, when the corporal and Gustof were returning from fishing, a patrol stopped them and took away their fish. The corporal said the soldiers did not realize he was Japanese. He knows this because the soldiers called them both monkeys. He laughed when he told me and seemed proud of his disguise: his ragged trousers and his dark skin.

***

Yesterday, when Armina had gone to the bath house, Santa motioned for me to come see the child. Her name is Mariko. She is very pretty, and I could not help saying so. At that, Santa scolded me, then she called out in a loud voice for the goblins: ugly child, very ugly child. This woke Mariko and she began crying. I hurried away before Armina returned.

Santa told me that Armina is afraid I will steal the child now that Uchida-san has taken me for his new wife. But I am not his wife and Santa must tell her that! Where would I take the child, I asked? Santa also told me that the night we first came here, Armina thought I was the ghost of Uchida-san's first wife. Such foolishness, and yet, I dare not trouble Uchida-san by mentioning the matter. Surely, he must know.

***

Today, when Mrs. Okata sent me to retrieve her *geta* from the leaving place in the front entrance, I noticed large spider webs hanging from the ceiling. I despise spiders and quickly ran to get a broom to dispose of them. I guess they felt free to move in because we so rarely use the front entrance.

Mrs. Okata spends a long time each day at the governor general's grave. She says she wonders at their touching sleeves, given the differences in their stations in life.

***

Many days with no rain. I sit at the Go board with Mrs. Okata, but she says I am hopeless. Sometimes Uchida-san joins her, sometimes the corporal when he and Gustof do not go fishing. She says the corporal is a better student than I am.

Gustof hides the boat in a different place now, and he and the corporal walk up the other side of the river to avoid the patrols. The river is low, they can cross over not far above the house. To bathe, we must wade out to the middle to find a deep pool, but then there are no rocks to sit on.

***

Uchida-san says breadfruit is related to the mulberry. When harvested, the fruit is hard and green, and though it is large and coarse looking, the shape is similar to a mulberry. Also, the sap is white and sticky. Santa chops it in half with a large cleaver, then into smaller pieces and puts them to steam in a large pot on a fire outside the kitchen. The cooking takes a long time. Then she peels it, slices it, and sprinkles it with *shoyu*. She worries that the *shoyu* will soon be gone.

Breadfruit is called *mahi*. A knife is *naip*. I spend most days, when it is not raining, in the garden where there is always some chore to be done, some vegetable or fruit to be harvested. I wear my *yukata* tied under my arms, and when I am sure no one will see me I go bare-breasted like a native woman.

***

At the forty-ninth day observations, Uchida-san spoke of the governor general's accomplishments and of the days before the military, a difficult but hopeful time for the early colonists. For someone of such few words, he talked at great length.

Uchida-san must miss the governor general and the time they spent together, often looking at maps like boys playing some game, the islands like Go stones scattered across the blue. Pointing, discussing. Will the Americans come here; will they go there? And the Imperial Navy,

which island lagoon conceals our ships
this week?

***

The news of the governor general's
death has traveled, and a message came
that the corporal must rejoin the other
soldiers. Santa washed and pressed the
remnants of his uniform and when he left,
he wore a pair of Uchida-san's trousers
with the cuffs rolled. Mrs. Okata trimmed
his hair.

When I look at the picture of my
brothers, I realize the corporal had become
as much of a brother to me as they were.
Remembering the first night we came to
this house, of going down to the river to
bathe and Mrs. Okata coming to tell us to
be quiet. The corporal and I were behaving
like children, she said, splashing each
other and making all kinds of noise. We

were so happy to be safe in the countryside.

***

A dream of giant silkworms. Not up in the attic like at my parent's house, or in the rafters of the barn like at elder brother's, but here, up in the trees, spinning giant cocoons so that the trees appeared decorated with hundreds of paper lanterns.

A sky filled with floating parachutes. Not another dream but imagining what it might look like when the Americans come. Uchida-san says they cannot come through the mangrove swamps. He says when they come, they will sail into the harbor and step ashore like tourists.

***

No rain for almost a week so every morning I carry water to the pumpkin plants. Santa has shown me the difference between the male and female flowers, how to remove the male flowers and rub them against the female ones.

Armina is wrong not to trust me. I am not Uchida-san's new wife. I mean no harm to her and her beautiful child. Does she believe I could refuse Uchida-san's wishes? That I have any choice?

***

Yesterday Santa came to the main room and asked to speak to Uchida-san. Mrs. Okata asked if she would like us to leave, but Santa said no. She then announced in a loud voice that the rice was gone. We have no more, she said. Her manner was comical, but the matter is serious. Mrs. Okata and I were embarrassed and buried our heads in our needlework.

At the time Uchida-san said nothing, but this morning he sent Gustof to the plantations, far to the east and south, to barter for rice. He is also to stop at the coconut plantations for cooking oil. For trade he is to use vegetables and what is left of the governor general's *sake*.

***

Only light rains, but already the river is growing. Uchida-san says he had thought of building a small dam and making a miniature hydroelectric plant to operate ceiling fans and maybe a few lights. Then he decided against it because the naval headquarters is not that far, only just west of the river mouth, and someone there might learn of it. Uchida-san says he does not wish for another visit from them.

Mrs. Okata has a bad toothache. Santa has given her some crushed leaves to put on it and she says it has helped some. Her jaw is swollen. For two days we have been awaiting Gustof's return.

***

The native workers have deserted the plantations, so the rice has not been harvested and what little Gustof brought has not been processed. When Santa inspected it, she pronounced it not fit to eat and said Gustof had traded for trash. Uchida-san sent Mrs. Okata to the kitchen to explain to Santa that only the color is different, that the rice is still good.

Uchida-san is very gloomy, no doubt looking into the future to an empty rice chest. What Gustof brought will not last long.

***

Gustof says people are hungry because the soldiers come with guns and take their food. He saw no dogs at all. Soon they will be eating cats. Santa remembers another time when people were hungry, a time when a terrible typhoon came with powerful winds that blew away houses and uprooted trees. The island was naked, and people starved.

Santa was only a small child and the memory is not strong, but something she heard spoken of for many years. This was also the time that people from the southern atolls came to the main island in large numbers. On the atolls, no trees remained at all, only sandy places and the lagoons. Armina's family was from one of the southern atolls.

***

From the south wing comes the sound of weeping. Not the child, the child hardly ever cries. I dared to ask Uchida-san if something is wrong, but he says she cries over nothing. How can it be for nothing? Is it that she feels like an autumn fan?

The mornings have been cool, but always the afternoons, hot. Too hot to sleep, too hot even for talk. Cannot Uchida-san assure her that she has not been discarded?

***

Gustof has been cutting bamboo. It is then trimmed and stacked. Uchida-san says he has a plan for it and sits at the table drawing and thinking for hour after hour, pausing only to wipe the dampness off his glasses on his sleeve.

I remember how elder brother spent the long winter months reading books, not speaking and no one daring to speak to him, his eyes unseeing when he looked up, as though the books had taken him to some distant land from which he had no wish to return.

***

Gustof took the cart up the steep path above the hydroelectric plant to harvest large bamboo. To believe how much he was able to load onto the cart, one would have to have seen it. Uchida-san is very mysterious about the purpose.

Still the weeping sounds, though one evening I heard her voice from the high window of the bath house, singing children's songs. Perhaps songs Mrs. Okata taught her? I asked Mrs. Okata but she said she had heard nothing, no singing, no weeping.

***

Now, when Gustof returns from fishing, there is barely enough for the evening meal because he has traded with people for hibiscus cord and pandanus leaves. The leaves are stacked in the main room, filling the whole south side, and Gustof keeps bringing more. Santa says it can only be for making thatch. But we have no need for thatch.

Uchida-san sits with his plans and says nothing.

***

The pandanus is for thatch, a thatch roof to go above the metal one. It will soften the sound of the rain and will make the house cooler. A clever plan and Uchida-san seems pleased with himself, but Santa says weaving is hard work and will take many weeks. Then she showed us how.

First, a length of hibiscus cord is attached to a small stick and the stick placed beneath the toes, then, the pandanus leaves are looped over the cord one by one and the cord knotted to hold them in place. Tomorrow we start.

***

Already, Mrs. Okata has blisters and can no longer help. Still, we are not halfway done. Gustof has built several ladders and is now covering the roof with a bamboo lattice to which the thatch will be attached.

The dust from the pandanus is itchy. There are cramps in my neck and shoulders, fits of coughing from the dust. Santa mimics my coughing and tells me that is what Uchida's wife died from. She must mean tuberculosis. It was at that time that Armina became part of the household, to help care for the young son whose name is Shige. Armina also spent many hours with Uchida's wife who told her stories until she could no longer speak from the coughing. Santa says Armina's head is filled with foolish fairy tales.

***

Gustof has begun attaching the thatch, layering it towards the roof peak. Uchida-san at the top of the ladder, Mrs. Okata at the bottom, and me in the middle, handing the thatch up. We should be finished in a few days. My hands are stiff, my fingers too sore to write anymore.

***

Today I saw the child again. Mrs. Okata was feeding her a mush of ripe bananas and coconut water. She resembles those beautiful dolls in fancy department stores. A round face with a

83

fringe and cap of dark hair, and flower-petal lips reaching for the spoon like a hungry carp.

Only light rains since the roof was completed. Uchida-san says the whole thing could blow off in a storm. He says that, but I don't think he believes it.

***

The rice is gone, the brown-colored rice Santa did not like. Uchida-san says another trip to the plantations would be useless as they had so little to spare before. Rice can be lived without, Santa said, as long as there are fish in the lagoon and a garden of fruits and vegetables. We also have chickens and their eggs.

Sometimes I feel as though we are living after the end of the world, as though something terrible has happened and only this island is left. Uchida-san has told me about the island before the military came, when there were only the natives and the colonists, of how hopeful everyone was, how happy their lives were. He says Japan will regret letting the military start this war with the Americans.

***

No noticeable seasons and little change in the length of days. But this snow I see? Only that the pods of the *kapok* tree have burst, and the wind spreads the white fluff over the countryside. So much, that I can gather small handfuls where it accumulates at the base of rocks and trees.

When I asked Santa if we could go to the *kapok* trees themselves and gather *kapok* for pillows and such, she said the *kapok* trees are like coconuts. But they are not alike at all, I said. She meant that the land they grow on belongs to someone else. All land belongs to someone, she said, only the sea is for everyone.

***

Santa has told me that no one lives in the mountains because of the dragons. But Uchida-san says the story of dragons is greatly exaggerated, that if there are any, they are merely large lizards.

I wondered if the mountains were like the sea and the lagoon and belong to everyone. Gustof, when consulted, said a trip into the mountains would take more than two days. Since I am not allowed to go to the lagoon, I did not bother to ask. Impossible, I would be told, not a trip for a woman.

***

People come to the kitchen begging for food. Others come in the night and steal pumpkins and papayas from the garden. Uchida-san has told Santa to be generous, to trade or give away all we can spare.

I asked Santa if we could trade some *kimonos* and sashes, I never wear, for *kapok*. People are hungry, she said, they do not need pretty things. Nor do we need *kapok*. There are plenty of cushions. I did not tell her I wanted it because it reminds me of snow.

***

A strong wind has come up. The tops of the mimosas are waving furiously and the bamboo at the very front of the house is flattened against the window screens. Gustof has gone to close the outside shutters, and Santa is busy cooking because if the storm is bad, she will not be able to light the fire. Tonight, she says, we will feast.

87

The table and cushions have been removed from the main room. Uchida-san says the storm will be a test for the new roof.

***

The thatch held. Mrs. Okata and I slept through the night as though there was no storm at all. But this morning, when Uchida-san came scratching at the *fusuma*, he was completely wet, even though the walkway is covered. The main room was awash with water.

Uchida-san changed into a dry *yukata*, then he and Mrs. Okata set up the Go board and settled down to play. When the rains softened, I went to bring us something from the kitchen. Santa had managed to light a small fire and she gave me hot tea and cold yam cakes. The tea, of course, is no longer real tea but some plant that grows here.

Small branches and leaves litter the yard and the chickens are missing. The river has risen. Until it recedes, it would be too dangerous to bathe.

I have been hearing weeping again. Santa says the people of the southern atoll where Armina's family was from have English blood. Over a century ago, some pirates killed all the men and lived for a time with the women. Santa says in the dialect of that southern atoll numbers are still counted in English.

***

Santa makes a paste of taro. It is not so bad when she makes it into little balls and fries it, but the supply of cooking oil is low. I long for the return of breadfruit season.

Such a muddy place, the taro patch, a muddy place below the bath house. Harvesting a taro with two people is not difficult, but it is for only one. I must dig down to expose the top of the root, then take hold of the stem and pull. I wedge a large stick against the root and push down on it with one foot. Yesterday I slipped and fell several times before the root gave way. What a muddy mess I was.

***

Again, Uchida-san sits at the table drawing plans. He is mysterious about them as before. When he stops to think, he pushes his glasses up on his head or takes them off and cleans them on his sleeve, over and over, so that I fear he is rubbing the glass away.

An embarrassing incident: Mrs. Okata coming down to the river when Uchida-san and I thought we were alone.

She never bathes in the river. Very strange.

***

Uchida-san's plans were not so grand this time, only a bamboo frame above a fire pit for smoking fish and seaweed. Smoked fish is tasty and will be a nice change.

It has been a long time since the last bombing. People have been moving in from the countryside. There are now several camps of them on the other side of the river. Gustof has noticed the disappearance of some banana stalks and a few small taros from the far edge of the garden.

***

Coming back from harvesting a yam which also takes much digging,

91

though not in mud like taro. The spindly vines are small evidence of how large the root can be. I was carrying back a yam the size of a man's head, when down the road came Uchida-san and Mariko. He was holding her hand and making his steps small to match hers. He told her to bow, to say hello, and held out her tiny hand for me to shake. I put the yam down, but my hands were too dirty. Next time, he said, then he lifted her up and carried her back to the house.

Santa says Armina becomes upset when anyone takes the child from the room. Yet, the child must have air and sun, she cannot live forever in a small room.

***

Telling only Santa we were going, I went with Gustof to the lagoon. He gave me a basket and I was to walk on the reef and look for seaweed and such. The tidepools were alive with all kinds of strange things. It has been so long since I had seen the sea that I had almost forgotten that this land is an island. The sparkle of sunlight on the pale lagoon water, then the white pencil-thin line of the waves breaking on the outer reef, and above a sky so large it almost took my breath away.

As I expected, a scolding from Mrs. Okata on our return, a scolding for us both. Even Uchida-san was quite severe. But I am determined to go with Gustof again.

***

Armina's voice calling for Mari-chan. The child had escaped, running like a drunk the length of the south walkway, through the main passage and then down the north walkway to the bath house.

Armina calling pitifully the whole time, until Santa caught up with the child and returned her.

I had feared being confined in that small room may have made her weak, but she seems as strong and lively as any child her age.

***

Santa has been hearing rumors from the people who come to the kitchen that the war is over. When she told Uchida-san, Mrs. Okata and I were both present. If the rumor is true, then Japan has lost. With no guns celebrating, how could it be otherwise. Uchida-san said nothing.

When he left the room, Mrs. Okata put her head down on the table and her shoulders began to shake, but I did not stay to comfort her. Feeling both a great relief and a great fear, I went down to the river to be alone with my thoughts.

***

Soon the Americans will come. Santa says that if the natives had pigs, they would be killed and roasted in celebration. Santa longs for the taste of roasted pork.

And what of us? Uchida-san says the islands will be taken as the spoils of war. And then, what will happen? What will it be like when we return? Will my brothers be alive? How can I return to my parents, to my village, after my shame?

***

Mrs. Okata whispered to me again of her nightmare, of a black cloud sucking the breath from every living thing. She wishes we had never left Nagasaki. There, she says, we would have been safe.

Yes, we would have been safe in Nagasaki, but I am not sorry we came here. Everything has been better since Mrs. Okata closed the doors of the brothel. I think of the older ones, like Chikako, and imagine that I, too, would have eventually taken to drink, given in to the momentary relief it offers, but hastening the path to old age and misery.

***

The Americans have not yet come. Most days we forget our fears. There is always work, some chore or other, to distract us.

Mrs. Okata is now thinking about the wire mesh screens which Uchida-san says are normally replaced every two years or three years. The ones in the main room are badly rusted and in places there are large holes. Mrs. Okata wants to cover the holes with pieces of silk. I do not care for this project. What is the use if we are leaving soon, or if they intend to kill us all, as Mrs. Okata whispers, they might?

***

I help to cut and hem pieces of silk for Mrs. Okata's foolish project. We use the bamboo ladders Gustof built for the thatching. With me on the outside and Mrs. Okata on the inside holding the pieces in place, we pass the needle from one side to the other.

Mrs. Okata says she plans to open a small business. A candy store or a noodle shop. She says if I decide not to return to my parents' house, she would let me have the room above her shop. I know what that means. Earning my keep the same way as before. I cannot bear the thought of that. Still, I thanked her for thinking of me. Yet, what other life can I expect?

***

Gustof has seen large ships outside the lagoon. The Americans will soon land. Mrs. Okata wants to hide, to flee into the mountains. Her mood is constantly changing. Several days ago, I watched her smoothing her hair back. She can make a tiny roll at the nape. She said she was thinking she might get a finger wave when she returns. Remembering the fuss she made when the others did that, I was unable to hide my amusement.

Of course, I am as apprehensive as she is. Don't we always fear what we do not know.

***

Yesterday Uchida-san went to see someone at the old naval headquarters and was told that first the soldiers are to be transported back to the home islands, then the colonists.

Gustof has not been fishing for several days. He is disturbed by all the American ships. One is inside the harbor, and two more outside the reef. Today I harvested another large yam.

***

This morning we heard the noise of a vehicle coming up the road. It was the Americans and they took Uchida-san away. Armina was upset and she frightened the child with her cries. Mrs. Okata went to calm her and sent Mari-chan to me. I took her to play by the river edge.

It was not long before Uchida-san returned. The Americans had taken him to

99

the hydroelectric plant. He laughed at our fears, saying the Americans would not bother to shoot a mere engineer. Still, I felt he was hiding some grave concern.

***

Uchida-san described the Americans to us. A gruff captain with no manners and a fearfully red face, and his translator, a young lieutenant who is most frightfully tall. From the young lieutenant Uchida-san learned that when the colonists are repatriated, they will not be allowed to take their native wives and children.

Uchida-san told this to Mrs. Okata and myself in confidence. He added that he believes exceptions will be made, that some highly skilled colonists will be needed and be allowed to stay. Like those who operate the canneries and oversee the plantations and himself who operates the hydroelectric plant.

***

The Americans came again and took Uchida-san to the hydroelectric plant where he learned it will not be reactivated. Instead, the Americans will set up their own generators for which they will bring in fuel. Uchida-san says it is utter foolishness to do that when water is something the island has in abundance. The dry season lasts only a short while, though it seems forever when one is suffering through it.

Without the hydroelectric plant being activated, Uchida-san will not be allowed to stay on. For that matter, he was told no Japanese will be allowed to stay on. Perhaps it is fortunate he did not have to make the choice himself, forced to choose between his son and his wife and their child. I have never told him of the ship being diverted to Saipan.

***

Armina is dead. It was Gustof who found her this morning at the river edge. The body has been placed in the south wing. Her face, that in life was said to be so beautiful, is now too terrible to look upon. Santa is cleaning the red *kimono* so she can be buried in it.

To put her face into the water and leave it there until her spirit departed, only minutes, but how long it must have felt as she fought against the body's desire for life. Impossible to imagine such courage, or such despair.

***

Now a second pile of stones. Uchida-san walks back and forth on the road in front of the house, carrying the child, hour after hour until finally Mari-chan begins to cry and someone goes and takes her from him.

Otherwise, life goes on as before. Chores to be done. The sun rises and sets. It rains, or it doesn't rain. More and more, I notice those small crimson-colored birds flitting through the garden. Yes, that same crimson red.

***

Mari-chan is enjoying the freedom of both the house and the yard and does not appear to miss her mother. When she stumbles and falls in the course of learning of steps and rocks, she calls out mama, as if she considers any of us -- Santa, Mrs. Okata or myself -- her mother, and whoever is closest runs to her aid.

Uchida-san stays by himself and says very little.

***

All but a few of the military have left and the colonists have been brought in from the countryside to await transport. Uchida-san says we will tell the American authorities that Mariko is our child and, when we reach Japan, I am to become his wife.

Mrs. Okata says how fortunate I am, but I am sure the Uchida family will not welcome me. I suspect they will know I have not come from bride's school and will guess I have been a brothel worker. I do not believe they will accept me or Mariko and her darker colored skin. Still, what is the alternative? For me to go with Mrs. Okata and work above her candy shop and the child to remain here with Santa and Gustof? They are already old.

***

Rain last night and everything smells musty. The bedding must be properly aired. I find a million things to do to keep me busy. I cannot explain what I do not truly understand myself. I only know that I must do this.

Mrs. Okata says I am being foolish. Uchida-san says only what an odd person I am and cautions me to truly consider the meaning of my decision. Santa and Gustof seem relieved and say there will be no problem keeping the secret. Santa whispered to me that there will be others who will go into hiding to stay here with their families.

***

This morning the noisy American jeep came up the road and stopped at the entrance. Mari-chan and I were down by the river. Soon I could hear their voices, feel their eyes. Uchida-san and the tall young lieutenant in the main room, their shadows looking down at us through the screen of patchwork silk. I heard the young lieutenant say: two days, that in two days all the Japanese nationals will have to enter the camp to await boarding the transport ship back to Japan.

Is that the woman, I heard him ask? Yes, Uchida-san answered, Armina and her child. And then he asked the American to please visit here often. In other words, he has given me to him. Mrs. Okata says I need not put it that way. As usual, she is practical. She says I will learn to speak English quickly.

***

Uchida-san told us the young lieutenant was surprised when he saw we have a metal roof under the thatch. In the district center the Americans are tearing down almost all the remaining Japanese houses and buildings. The young lieutenant assured Uchida-san that he will tell no one about this house.

This morning I helped Mrs. Okata pack. They are allowed only a small bundle each. Now Uchida-san is burning papers and I am to give him my notebook. Then Armina will be reborn and Mieko will be truly gone. Tonight, a wet pillow is to be expected.

Guide to Characters and Terms

Armina, local wife of Mr. Uchida

Bento, Japanese boxed lunches

Chikako, oldest Ifumi brothel worker

Fusuma, decorated opaque sliding screen

Futon, Japanese mattress/bed

Geta, elevated wooden sandal

Go, popular board game

Gustof, servant & husband of Santa

Mr. Ito, one of Mieko's schoolteachers

Igo, a garçon or servant boy

Izumi, fellow Ifumi worker, good dancer

Josefa, Ifumi brothel cook & housekeeper

Kapok, natural fibers for pillow stuffing

Kimiko/Kimi-chan, Mieko's best friend

Kimono, traditional Japanese garment

Ifumi, Mieko's brothel

Mariko/Mari-chan, Armina's daughter

Mieko/Mieko-chan, narrator of Miss Gone-overseas

Namiki dori, main shopping street

Ohmine, western part of town

Oichi, Kimiko's brothel

Pandanus, sturdy-leafed local plant

Mrs. Okata, manager of Ifumi brothel

Sake, rice wine

Santa, servant & wife of Gustof

Sefina, Josefa's daughter

Shoyu, Japanese soy sauce

Mr. Shimba, geta shop & parrot owner

Sumiko, fellow Ifumi brothel worker

Sutras, Buddhist texts

Mr. Uchida/Uchida-san, the engineer

Tatami, grass mat flooring, approx. 3' x 6'

Yukata, light-weight cotton kimono

Yukio, an Ifumi brothel worker

3-Mat room, about 6 x 9 feet

6-Mat room, about 9 x 12 feet

12-Mat room, about 12 x 18 feet

ABOUT THE AUTHOR

For a number of years in the 1980s, Mitchell Hagerstrom lived and worked on the island of Pohnpei in Micronesia where this story takes place. She now lives in Austin, Texas. For more information, visit her at the *Miss Gone-overseas* pages on Facebook, Goodreads, and Amazon.

Other books by Mitchell:

Overseas Stories, sequel to Miss Gone-Overseas, original Kindle version 1st Edition 2012 published by Tiny Toe Press, re-vised Kindle 2nd Edition 2019 published by Penryn Editions.

Gathered Pieces, collection of short stories 2019, Published by Penryn Editions.

Made in the USA
Lexington, KY
17 September 2019